SHAKE dem Halloween Bones

W. Nikola-Lisa

Illustrated by Mike Reed

Houghton Mifflin Company
Boston

www.hmco.com/trade

Library of Congress Cataloging-in-Publication Data

Shake dem Halloween bones / by W. Nikola-Lisa; illustrated by Mike Reed.
p. cm.
Summary: A rhythmic tale about different fairy tale characters
who attend a hip-hop Halloween ball.
RNF ISBN 0-395-73095-3   PAP ISBN 0-618-07034-6
[1. Characters and characteristics in literature — Fiction. 2. Halloween — Fiction.
3. Balls (Parties) — Fiction. 4. Stories in rhyme.] I. Reed, Mike, 1951–   ill. II. Title.
PZ8.3.N5664Sh 1997
[E] — dc20 94-49738 CIP AC
Manufactured in the United States of America
BVG 10 9 8 7

To Nikki Sue and Scout,
who really know how to shake it.
— W.N-L.

To Jane, Alex, and Joe
— M.R.

It's Halloween night.
Jack-o'-lanterns glow in darkened windows.
Goblins crouch behind front-porch stoops.
Witches peer from nearby rooftops.

The city is quiet. *The city is still.*

But as the lights go down, the music comes up —

ah-one,
ah-two,
ah-one,
two,
three,
four...

Shake, shake,
    shake dem bones now.
Shake, shake,
    shake dem bones now.
Shake, shake,
    shake dem bones
at the hip-hop Halloween ball.

Hey, Li'l Red, so sweet, so good,
 you sure can shake that ridin' hood.
Come on, Li'l Red, won't you dance with me
 at the hip-hop Halloween ball?

Now here comes Jack with a cow to sell.
Did you ever think Jack could dance so well?
Come on, Li'l Jack, won't you dance with me
at the hip-hop Halloween ball?

I said, *shake, shake, shake dem bones now.*
Shake, shake, shake dem bones now.
Shake, shake, shake dem bones
at the hip-hop Halloween ball.

Tom Thumb's a-rockin'; he's a-shakin' dem bones.
For a tiny little guy, he can shake it on home.
Come on, Li'l Tom, won't you dance with me
at the hip-hop Halloween ball?

Snow White is here in a fancy dress,
with seven little men, no more, no less.
Come on, Li'l Snowy, won't you dance with me
at the hip-hop Halloween ball?

Now, look at Goldilocks
    a-twirlin' those bears.
No wonder she busted
    their rockin' chairs.
Come on, Li'l Goldie,
    won't you dance with me
at the hip-hop Halloween ball?

I said, *shake, shake, shake dem bones now.*
Shake, shake, shake dem bones now.

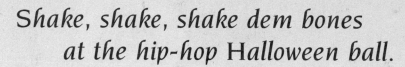

Shake, shake, shake dem bones
at the hip-hop Halloween ball.

Hey, Mister Pig, dancin' all alone,
did you chase that wolf
from your fine brick home?
Come on, Sweet Pig,
won't you dance with me
at the hip-hop Halloween ball?

Rapunzel, Rapunzel, let your hair hang down.
Come out of your tower and shake it all around.
Come on, Li'l 'Punzel, won't you dance with me
at the hip-hop Halloween ball?

I said, *shake, shake, shake dem bones now.*
Shake, shake, shake dem bones now.
Shake, shake, shake dem bones
at the hip-hop Halloween ball.

Rumpelstiltskin, you're so mean.
Spinnin' straw into gold nearly tricked the queen.
Come on, Li'l 'Stiltskin, won't you dance with me
at the hip-hop Halloween ball?

Hey, Cinderella, it's a quarter to twelve.
　　You better get shakin' 'fore they ring that bell.
Come on, Li'l 'Rella, won't you dance with me
　　at the hip-hop Halloween ball?

The last one's Puss with his big ol' boots.
He's stompin' the floor and a-shakin' the roof.
Come on, Big Puss, won't you dance with me
at the hip-hop Halloween ball?

I said, *shake, shake, shake dem bones now.*
Shake, shake, shake dem bones now.

Shake, shake, shake dem bones
at the hip-hop Halloween ball.

One more time . . .

I said, *shake, shake, shake dem bones now.*
Shake, shake, shake dem bones now.
Shake, shake, shake dem bones
at the hip-hop Halloween ball.

AT THE HIP-HOP HALLOWEEN BALL!

Scoo-bee-doo-bee-doo-wah.

Yeah!